15.95

15.95

THE BREMEN TOWN MUSICIANS

THE BREMEN TOWN MUSICIANS

retold from the Brothers Grimm
and illustrated by JANET STEVENS

Holiday House / New York

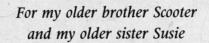

Library of Congress Cataloging-in-Publication Data
Stevens, Janet.
The Bremen town musicians / adapted from the Brothers Grimm
and illustrated by Janet Stevens.
p.   cm.
Summary: A retelling of the Grimm tale in which an old donkey,
dog, cat, and rooster, no longer wanted by their masters,
set out for Bremen to become musicians.
ISBN 0-8234-0939-2
[1. Fairy tales.   2. Folklore—Germany.]
I. Bremer Stadtmusikanten. English.   II. Title.
PZ8.S614Br   1992   91-815   CIP   AC
398.2—dc20
[E]

To create the illustrations for this book,
Janet Stevens used mixed media, including
gouache, pastels, and ink, on handmade paper.
The paper was fabricated out of rice straw and
Russian hemp by Ray Tomasso.

Once upon a time, there lived a donkey who was old and tired. He could no longer carry heavy loads to the mill.

"I am so weak, I know my master will soon get rid of me," he said. "I'm going to run away." The donkey hobbled out of town as fast as his bony legs would go.

"I need to find a new career," he thought as he walked along. "A lute player doesn't have to be strong. I will go to Bremen and become the town musician."

A little while later, the donkey stumbled over an old hound in the road who was gasping for breath.

"What's wrong with you?" asked the donkey.

The hound moaned, "I am so old and tired, I can't hunt anymore. My master wanted to do away with me, so I left. Here I am, with no money or food."

"Cheer up!" exclaimed the donkey. "Why don't you join me? I am traveling to Bremen to play as the town musician. Will you come? I will play the lute and you the kettle drum. We will make a fine Bremen town band."

The hound barked "Yes!" so the two hobbled off down the road.

After they had walked a few miles, the donkey and the hound met a cat. She looked scraggly and bedraggly and most upset.

"What's your problem, old cat?" asked the donkey and the hound.

"My time is almost up," whined the cat. "My teeth are gone, and I can't catch mice. My mistress was about to drown me, so I ran away. Now here I lie, hungry and penniless."

"Don't worry," said the donkey and the hound. "Come with us. We are traveling to Bremen to be town musicians. Your meow would sound nice in our band."

The cat smiled a toothless smile, and the three animals set off down the road.

They had not traveled far when they heard a rooster crowing.

"Why does your crow sound so sad?" asked the three animals.

"I am very old," he said. "My master wants rooster soup for his dinner. Tonight he plans to cook me."

"Don't worry, old rooster. Come join our band. We are going to Bremen to become town musicians. Your cock-a-doodle-doo would add fine high notes to our music."

"Anything's better than the soup pot," said the rooster. He flew down from his perch and joined the travelers.

So the four animals continued down the road to Bremen. Their bones creaked and their muscles ached as they shuffled along.

By nightfall they had not reached the town.

"I'm so tired I could sleep standing up!" groaned the donkey.

"I'm so hungry I could eat a horse," moaned the dog.

"Perhaps we should stop for the night," said the cat. "The ground is hard on my brittle old bones." Far off she could see a light flickering in a farmhouse. "Why don't we stop at that house and look for a comfortable bed and something to eat?" she suggested.

They all agreed that this was a good idea and limped toward the flickering light.

When the four arrived at the house, the donkey peeked through the window.

"What do you see, donkey?" the others asked.

"I see a glorious table laden with fine food and drink. But I also see robbers eating the feast." His stomach growled. "How I wish that supper were ours."

"Shhh," the hound warned. "Let's think of a plan to drive those robbers away."

The animals talked late into the night. Finally, they came up with an idea.

First the donkey stood on his hind legs. Then the hound slowly crawled up onto his back. The cat struggled to balance on top of the dog. The rooster flew up and landed on the cat's head.

They looked in the window and began to perform their music.

"**Hee-haw**," brayed the donkey.

"**Yowl-l-l-l**," sang the hound.

"**Meow**," went the cat.

"**Cock-a-doodle-doo**," crowed the cock.

At that moment, the stack of animals teetered and tottered and fell forward, crashing through the window.

"Yikes! A ghost!" cried the robbers. "Let's get out of here!" And they ran away, deep into the forest.

After the four musicians recovered from the crash, they picked themselves up.

"Let's eat," brayed the donkey.

"I want that beef bone," barked the dog.

"Where's the milk?" meowed the cat.

"That corn looks good," crowed the rooster.

The animals dove into the food and ate until their stomachs were full.

"I'm ready for bed," said the cat. She stretched out on the warm hearth.

"Me too," said the hound. He curled up on the mat behind the door.

The donkey yawned. "I'll go make a bed out of straw in the yard."

"I'll sleep up on the roof," said the rooster, and he flew after him.

The animals fell asleep as the fire died out.

Far away, the robbers could see that the house was dark. "The ghost must be gone," said the first robber.

"Let's go back and finish our dinner," said the second.

"But what if the ghost is only asleep?" said the third. The men decided to send the first robber ahead to see if the ghost was still there.

He crept up the road to the house. He tiptoed through the door and into the kitchen. It was cold and dark, so he lit a candle. Then, mistaking the gleaming eyes of the cat for hot coals, he knelt down to light them.

The cat scratched and spit.

The robber fell back and landed on the dog, who promptly bit his leg.

The robber dashed out the door and tripped over the donkey, who kicked him hard.

The cock swooped down, screeching, "Cock-a-doodle-doo."

"This house is *really* haunted!" yelled the robber. He ran back to the forest as fast as he could.

When he reached the other robbers, he cried, "A terrible witch has taken over the house. She spat in my face and scratched me with her horrible long claws. As I ran out the door, a ghost stabbed me in the leg with a knife. In the yard a scary, dark monster hit me with a club while up on the roof a judge screamed, 'Bring the rogue to me! Bring the rogue to me!' We can't return to that dreadful haunted house."

The robbers didn't go back, and that suited the four
friends just fine. Even though they never reached Bremen
to become town musicians, they lived out their remaining
years in peace and happiness.